Growing Cotton

Heather Hammonds

Chapter 1

Cotton Plants

These clothes are all made from cotton.

Did you know that cotton comes from cotton plants?

Fluffy cotton **fibre** is part of the fruit of cotton plants.

Cotton fibre is made into **yarn**.

The yarn is made into fabric.

Other things can be made from cotton fibre too.

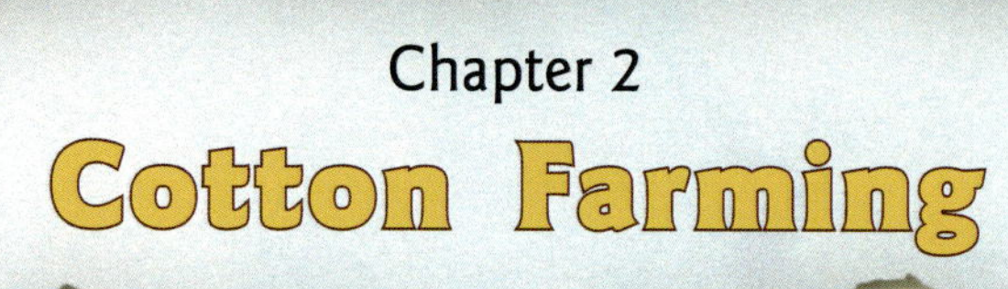

Chapter 2

Cotton Farming

Cotton plants grow best in places where it is hot in summer. They need good soil and water too.

Cotton plants are grown on cotton farms.
New cotton plants are planted every year.

Farmers work hard to care for the cotton plants.
When the plants grow well,
they make lots of cotton!

It takes about six months for cotton plants to grow and make cotton.

Chapter 3

Planting Time

Cotton seeds are planted in the spring.

Before the seeds are planted,
the cotton fields are dug with big machines.

After the fields are dug, they are watered. On many cotton farms, water is pumped between rows of soil.

When the fields are ready, the cotton seeds are planted.

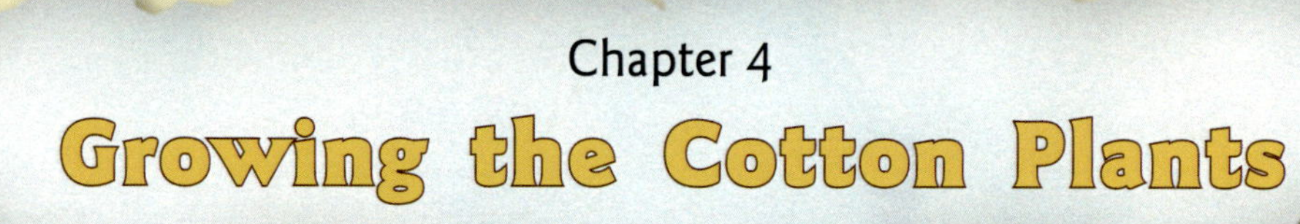

Chapter 4

Growing the Cotton Plants

Soon after planting, the cotton seeds begin to grow. The new plants are given more water. The fields are weeded too.

These farmers are weeding their field.

Cotton plants need plant food. Plant food is put into the water, or put into the soil.

Cotton farmers check their cotton plants to work out the best times to water them, weed them and give them plant food.

Chapter 5

Enemies!

Cotton plants have many enemies. Lots of insects like to eat them. Special **insect sprays** are sprayed on cotton crops to kill the insects.

a boll weevil

a bollworm

a harlequin bug

Diseases can also harm cotton plants.

Some cotton plants do not get many diseases. Farmers grow these kinds of cotton plants.

Weeds can spread diseases! Farmers work hard to keep weeds out of their cotton fields.

Chapter 6

Buds, Flowers and Bolls

When cotton plants are about five weeks old, they begin to grow little flower buds.

About four weeks later, the flower buds begin to open.

The flower petals soon fall off and the fruit of the cotton plant begins to grow.

The fruit of the cotton plant is called a **boll**.

Fluffy cotton fibre and cotton seeds grow inside cotton bolls.

Chapter 7

Harvest Time

It takes many weeks for the cotton bolls to grow.
Then when they are ready,
the bolls burst open.
They are full of cotton fibre and seeds!

a boll that has burst open

When all the bolls are open,
it is time to **harvest** the cotton.

Big machines harvest the cotton.
The cotton fibre and seeds are pulled off the cotton plants by the machines.

When the cotton has been harvested, it is pressed into huge blocks.

Huge blocks of cotton are called **modules**.

Chapter 8

At the Factory

The huge blocks of cotton are taken to a factory.

At the factory, cotton seeds are taken out of the fluffy fibre.

cotton seeds

Then the cotton fibre is cleaned.
Leaves, sticks and dirt are taken out of it.

The clean fibre is pressed into big **bales**.

A little bit of cotton from each bale is sent away and checked, to see how good it is.

Chapter 9

Cotton Seeds

Cotton seeds are a very important part of cotton farming.

They are made into food for people and animals.

animal food

cooking oil

Other things are made from cotton seeds too.

an x-ray

Some cotton seeds are not made into food or other things. They will be planted the next spring. They will grow into new cotton plants.

Chapter 10

From Fluff to Fabric

Cotton fibre is made into yarn at a cotton **mill**.

First the bales of cotton are cleaned again and mixed together.

Then big machines spin the cotton into **yarn**.

Now the yarn is ready to be made into fabric.

Big machines make the yarn into different kinds of fabric.

cotton fabric in a dress

Then the fabric is made into clothes for us to wear!

cotton fabric in jeans

Glossary

bales	large square sacks full of cotton, or other material such as wool
boll	the fruit of the cotton plant. Cotton grows inside the bolls.
diseases	sicknesses
fibre	a tiny thread of material, or group of tiny threads of material
harvest	to pick a crop of plants when they are ripe
insect sprays	special mixtures put on cotton plants in lots of tiny drops, to kill insects
mill	a factory where yarn or fabric is made
modules	huge square blocks of cotton
yarn	thread made from materials like cotton or wool that can be used to make fabric

Index